JAMAL'S INHERITANCE

The certified letter was propped up against the salt and pepper shakers on the kitchen table.

"Dear Jamal Jenkins," the letter began. "As you may or may not know, Bethany Franklin passed away last Saturday."

"What is it?" his mom asked.

"I don't know yet."

Then, suddenly, in his mind's eye Jamal remembered the old woman at the community center, remembered her mysterious words: "I have a plan."

"We must ask you to report to our offices this Saturday, April 23, at 4:00. At that time we will have the official reading of Bethany Franklin's will, and"—the next words froze his heart—"we will give you your inheritance. . . ."

Join the Team!

Do you watch GHOSTWRITER on PBS? Then you know that when you read and write to solve a mystery or unravel a puzzle, you're using the same smarts and skills the Ghostwriter team uses.

We hope you'll join the team and read along to help solve the mysterious and puzzling goings-on in these GHOSTWRITER books!

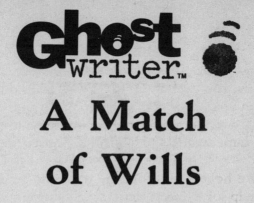

Ghost writer™

A Match of Wills

by

Eric Weiner

Illustrated by Eric Velasquez

**A
CHILDREN'S TELEVISION WORKSHOP
BOOK**

BANTAM BOOKS
NEW YORK • TORONTO • LONDON • SYDNEY • AUCKLAND

A MATCH OF WILLS

A Bantam Book / November 1992

Ghostwriter, **Ghost**writer and ◉
are trademarks of Children's Television Workshop.
All rights reserved. Used under authorization.

Art direction by Marva Martin
Cover design by Susan Herr
Interior illustrations by Eric Velasquez

ISBN 0-553-29934-4

Published simultaneously in the United States and Canada

Bantam Books are published by Bantam Books, a division of Bantam
Doubleday Dell Publishing Group, Inc. Its trademark, consisting of the
words "Bantam Books" and the portrayal of a rooster, is Registered
in U.S. Patent and Trademark Office and in other countries. Marca
Registrada. Bantam Books, 666 Fifth Avenue, New York, New York
10103.

PRINTED IN THE UNITED STATES OF AMERICA

OPM   0   9   8   7   6   5   4   3   2   1

ATTENTION, READER!

AS YOU READ THIS BOOK, PLEASE WATCH
FOR SIGNS LIKE THIS ONE...

THIS IS A SIGNAL THAT I NEED TO SPEAK
TO YOU.

AND YOU ALONE.

I PROMISE WE SHALL MEET AGAIN SOON!

—GHOSTWRITER

PROLOGUE

Mysterious Words

IT WAS MONDAY, AFTER SCHOOL. TWELVE year-old Jamal Jenkins had just added his initials to the list of top scorers on Zargon, the community center's video game. The top *four* scores all now said the same thing: "J.J."

He glanced at the tenth score, which was way behind his own. It said "Bethany." Jamal smiled and fished in his pocket for another quarter, but his hand came up empty.

As he sauntered out of the rec room, he heard a cheer coming from a room down the hall. He stuck his head in the door.

Inside, a group of kids clustered around one of the desks. What were they watching? He couldn't see. He worked his way closer.

"Hey, Jamal," said a girl's voice to his right. "You're just in time for the showdown."

Jamal turned and saw an eleven-year-old girl with brownish-blond hair and familiar, soft brown eyes. Lenni Frazier.

"Hey, Lenni." Jamal grinned. "What's going on?"

Lenni nodded in the direction of the desk. "Alex is playing for the championship of the chess club. Whoever wins this game is number one in the center."

"Go, Alex!" The cheer came from Gaby Fernandez, Alex's little sister. She was jumping up and down with excitement.

"Quiet!" someone hissed.

Gaby jumped up and down a couple more times. "Go, Alex," she whispered.

Jamal moved closer so he could see better. Alex was playing the dark pieces. His opponent was a short black woman whose full head of hair had turned completely gray. The woman was in her eighties, at least. She wore a dark overcoat, and across her lap lay an old cane with a silver lion's head handle.

"Bethany," said Jamal with a smile.

The old woman looked up from the chessboard. Her tiny eyes twinkled.

Now Alex looked up, as well. "Hey, Jamal," he teased, "I didn't know you were interested in a *real* game."

"It doesn't get any realer than Zargon," Jamal answered. "Chess is for eggheads, right, Bethany?"

Bethany answered with a wink. He winked back and said, "Alex, I hate to tell you this, but I think you're in trouble."

"Think again," Alex said, studying the board.

"What I mean is, Zargon is the *only* thing that I can win against this woman. When it comes to puzzles, she's the queen."

"Now, now," Bethany said, her eyes shining. "You better let your friend concentrate."

"Yes, let's keep it down," added Mr. Santana, the chess club supervisor. "The players need to think."

"Who is she?" Lenni whispered in Jamal's ear.

"She hangs around the center," Jamal whispered back. "I taught her how to play Zargon. So she's always giving me these wicked brain-teasers. She's really smart."

"She sure plays a mean game of chess," agreed Lenni. "I lost to her in about five minutes."

As the players took turns moving, Lenni whispered more comments. She explained the basic rules, how the pieces moved.

"Momo showed me once in the park," Jamal whispered back, "but it all just goes so slowly. It makes me itchy."

"Okay, so you know," whispered Lenni, "that the goal of the game is to trap the other person's king, right? That's called checkmate."

"Yeah."

"Jamal," whispered a voice.

Jamal smiled and nodded back at another one of the spectators, Tina Nguyen.

Now the old woman moved her queen. Her wrinkled hand shook as she moved the piece.

Jamal studied the board, trying to tell who was ahead. When he looked up, Bethany was smiling at him. "Here's a little puzzle for you," she said. "What do you think's about to happen?"

"I'm new to this game," Jamal said, peering at the board.

"What's about to happen . . ." Alex began, lifting his rook, "is bad news for you!"

He swept his rook all the way across the board, and captured his enemy's queen.

There was a round of applause from the spectators. Gaby was jumping up and down again. "All right!" she said.

"Way to go, Alex!" called Tina.

But the old woman only smiled. She was still looking at Jamal. "That was an ambush," she said quietly in her gravelly voice. "I *let* my opponent take off a piece. But that was a trap. Do you see why?"

Jamal stared at the board. The goal is to trap the other person's king, he reminded himself. Then, suddenly, he saw it.

By moving his rook to take the queen, Alex

had left his king all alone in the back row.

"You're going to bring your rook down," Jamal said.

The old woman burst into a grin. One of her teeth flashed silver. She clutched her cane as she got to her feet. "Exactly. You're hard to stump."

Now her wrinkled hand closed around her rook. "In this game," she told Alex and Jamal, "you have to stay one move ahead of your opponent. That's my secret."

She moved her rook to Alex's back row and plunked it down. "Checkmate," she said quietly.

Alex groaned. But then he stood up and held out his hand. "Good game," he said.

Mr. Santana made a note on his clipboard. "Well, kids," he said. "Looks like our newest member is also our club's new champion. Congratulations, Bethany. I hope we'll see you at lots more meetings."

"I hope so, too," she said with a tiny smile.

Mr. Santana swept the game pieces into a big bucket. The audience started to disperse. Alex's face was glum as he pulled on his jacket.

"Next time," Lenni told him.

"She tricked you," Gaby added.

"She sure did," Alex said. "But that's the point of the game."

"You guys want to get a slice?" Lenni suggested, glancing from Alex to Jamal.

"Sounds great!" Gaby answered. Alex looked

at his younger sister and rolled his eyes. "What?" said Gaby. "She was talking to me, too! Weren't you, Lenni?"

"Of course," Lenni assured her.

"Tina?" Gaby called. "Pizza?"

"You bet!"

"Count me in," Jamal said as he followed his friends out the door.

He was the last one out of the room. At least, he thought he was. Before he got out the door, though, a cold hand closed around his wrist.

It was Bethany.

"Just a second, Jamal," she said. He waited. "Tell me something. Why didn't you enter the tournament?" Bent over, leaning on her cane, the old woman was several inches shorter than the boy.

"I told you, I've never really played chess."

Bethany eyed him closely, as if she didn't believe him. "But you guessed my next move." She grinned. "I guess you're even smarter than I thought."

Jamal shrugged. "Thanks."

She still hadn't let go of his wrist. "Listen—" She lowered her already quiet voice.

"Jamal! You coming, or what?" Alex had stuck his head back in the door.

"In a second."

"My stomach is growling," Alex complained.

"In a second," Jamal repeated. "I promise."

"Listen, Bethany," he said, "I gotta go." He gently tried to pull his hand away, but her grip tightened. She was surprisingly strong.

"Just a second," she said. She stared at him closely, as if she were inspecting him. "I've been thinking about it for a long time, and I finally decided. I've got one last puzzle for you."

"Great!" he said. "But listen, can it wait till tomorrow? I—"

Bethany waved her hand impatiently. "I'm not going to give you the puzzle now."

"Oh?" Jamal shrugged. This seemed like a puzzle in itself.

He waited for her to go on, but she didn't say a word. Then, finally, she said, "I have a plan."

She said it so quietly, he almost didn't hear her. But she darted a look around the empty room to make sure they were really alone.

"That's all I can tell you right now," she added. "But remember. I have a plan."

Six Months Later...

MOMO PIVOTED TO HIS LEFT, DUCKED right, then made his move to the basket. Jamal jumped. But the taller teenager's lay-up whooshed past Jamal's outstretched fingertips. Jamal didn't need to turn and look. He heard the ball swish through the net behind him.

"That's all she wrote, bro," Momo told the other players as Jamal retrieved the ball. Momo strode over to CJ, the captain of Jamal's team. "We'd stay and beat you again, but I can't hang," Momo said. He raised his forearm in salute, and he and CJ banged their arms together.

The young players were heading off in all directions. "Better work on that hook shot," Momo called to Jamal with a grin, "if you want to make up for the way I *tower* over you."

"I'll get you next time," Jamal promised.

"In your dreams," said Momo. "Later."

Jamal watched as the tall boy headed away through the park, past the homeless people snoozing on the benches. Then he picked up his half-finished can of soda, took a swig, and started out of the park in the other direction. When he finished the soda, he hooked the empty can at a wire trash can, about twenty feet away. It landed without touching the rim.

"Now, why didn't I do that during the game?" Jamal asked himself, shaking his head.

"Jamal!"

He looked up. Just outside the park, a sturdy black woman in a blue post office uniform had her hand in the air, waving.

Still dribbling, Jamal broke into a loping trot across the cement pathway.

"Grandma!" he called when he got close. "Here comes Air Jenkins." He leapt and stuck his tongue out the way Michael Jordan did when he drove for the basket.

Cecilia Jenkins gave a deep belly laugh. "You may not be Air Jordan," she said. "But you sure are Air Mail. Or Certified, I should say."

"Huh?"

"You got a certified letter from some law firm. I signed for it. It's waiting on the kitchen table."

Jamal stared at her blankly. "*I* got a what?"

"A certified letter. That's a letter that the post

office guarantees gets delivered. It costs extra. Someone means business." CeCe narrowed her eyes. "Any idea why a law firm would want to get in touch with you?"

Jamal wiped his forehead with the back of his hand. "Nope."

He ran all the way home, the basketball tucked under one arm. The certified letter was propped up against the salt and pepper shakers on the kitchen table. There was a green form taped to the envelope, showing where his grandmother had signed. The return address read:

Kohegan, Stark, and Finn
Attorneys at Law

Jamal held up the envelope and tried to read the letter through the envelope.

"It helps if you open it," his mother said. She was standing in the kitchen doorway, holding a bag of groceries.

"Right." Jamal ripped open the envelope.

"Dear Jamal Jenkins," the letter began. "As you may or may not know, Bethany Franklin passed away last Saturday."

Bethany Franklin? The name meant absolutely nothing to him. He quickly ran through the kids in his class at Zora Neale Hurston Middle School. Bethany?

"What is it?" his mom asked.

"I don't know yet."

Suddenly, in his mind's eye he saw a cane with a silver lion's head handle. And then he remembered the old woman at the community center, remembered her mysterious words: "I have a plan." But that had been in the fall. Now it was spring. He hadn't seen her around the center in months, and he had forgotten all about her.

"We must ask you to report to our offices this Saturday, April 23, at 4:00. At that time we will have the official reading of Bethany Franklin's will, and"—the next words froze his heart—"we will give you your inheritance."

Jamal stared at the letter. "Mom? What's an inheritance?"

Mrs. Jenkins was loading the groceries into the fridge. "That's when someone leaves you money when they die," she said, filling the egg tray, "but dream on, son. Your father and I plan on sticking around for a long, long time, and there isn't any money, anyway."

"There is now," Jamal said.

"What?" Mrs. Jenkins turned to give him a look.

He dropped the letter. "Mom!" he suddenly yelled. "I'm rich!"

Mrs. Jenkins didn't move. "What are you talking about?"

He picked the letter up off the floor and showed it to her.

"I told you about Bethany, remember?"

"No."

"She's this lady I met at the community center. I taught her Zargon, and she used to give me these brainteasers. She told me she had a plan. Then I never saw her again. But don't you see? She must have been one of those crazy old rich ladies, and her plan was to give it all to me!"

He danced around the room, almost colliding with his grandmother as she entered the kitchen. "Whoah," she said. "You doing that Air Jordan stuff again?"

"Grandma," Jamal yelled. "I'm rich!"

"Now, wait a minute," his mother said. "Don't start getting your hopes up." But she was smiling, too, as she handed CeCe the letter.

"Well!" CeCe whistled after she read the letter.

"Rich! Rich! Rich!" Jamal clapped his hands, then opened an imaginary car door for himself. "Mr. Jenkins. Your limo..."

"Oh, Jamal," CeCe crooned, "you know you're my favorite grandson, don't you?"

Jamal laughed and started doing a moonwalk around the room.

"I'm your *only* grandson."

"My point exactly."

"Don't worry, Grandma. After I inherit my million dollars, you can have..."

He paused. CeCe raised her eyebrows.

"A dollar," Jamal said. Then he ran, because CeCe was chasing him.

It seemed as if it would never be Saturday. Jamal couldn't stop daydreaming about how he would spend his millions. He would buy the New York Knicks, and let himself play. He would set up a video arcade in his own room. He would buy a jet and fly around the world.

He didn't forget his friends, either. Since Lenni loved writing songs, he promised to buy her a sound studio, where she could record her work. He'd buy Tina all the best video equipment, for her school news team. He'd buy Alex a BMW with a chauffeur, so he could drive around the country and visit all those girls he was pen pals with. For Gaby, he promised a complete set of the *Encyclopaedia Britannica*. Of course, it often seemed like Gaby knew most of that stuff already, but she still seemed excited when he told her.

In fact, by the end of the week, all of his friends were almost as worked up as he was. And that Saturday, they all went with him to the law office.

It was a hot day, and the streets of Brooklyn were crowded. A storekeeper was hosing down the sidewalk in front of his bodega, and the five friends had to dodge around the stream of water.

"I've decided to give you something new," Jamal told Alex. "After I get my millions, I'm going to produce a movie for you to star in."

"Cool," said Alex. He clutched an imaginary collar on his T-shirt and strutted down the sidewalk. He waved at passersby, saying, "No autographs, no autographs."

Lenni applauded, but Gaby turned to Jamal and demanded, "What about me?"

"How about a mansion?" Jamal offered.

"Sounds good," Alex joked. "Especially if it's far away."

He ducked as Gaby swung her backpack at him.

Lenni pointed up and yelled, "There it is!"

The law office was on Greene Street, on the second floor, above a discount drugstore. Lawyer/Abogado, Cheap Divorce, read the sign. But the five kids stared up at the office window as if they expected dollar bills to flutter down on top of them any second.

Upstairs, the receptionist checked her clipboard and said, "Uh, Mr. Jenkins, yes, Mr. Kohegan is expecting you. He's in the conference room, which is down the hall on your left. But"—she looked at Lenni, Alex, Tina, and Gaby—"I'm afraid your friends are going to have to wait out here."

"It's okay," Lenni told him.

"We'll cross our fingers," Gaby said.

Jamal's ratty sneakers squeaked on the old wooden floor as he headed down the hall. Tomorrow, I'll buy new ones, he promised himself. Two pairs! He knocked on the conference room door.

"Come in."

When he opened the door, he saw a large, beefy man with a black-and-gray mustache. The man was staring back at him with small, angry eyes. The eyes looked somehow familiar.

"Mr. Jenkins, I presume," said a friendly voice to his left. He turned and saw a short, bald man in a three-piece suit, rising from his chair at the other end of the table. "Jason Kohegan." The man smiled kindly and held out a small hand. "Please call me Jason."

Jamal gripped the hand sideways in a power shake. "Oh, ah, yes," said the lawyer, looking flustered. "Jamal, this is Edward Franklin, Bethany Franklin's son."

So that's why those eyes had looked familiar!

Edward Franklin stood. He looked to be in his late fifties, and he must have been over six feet tall. He held out his hand and gave Jamal the hardest handshake he had ever felt. Edward's angry eyes stared into his. It was as if those eyes were saying, "Don't mess with me."

Jason put his glasses on and peered down at the papers before him. "Well," he said, "I'm sure you both are anxious to get on with this."

"It's so crazy having this kid here," Edward growled, still staring at Jamal.

"Well, now," the lawyer answered gently, "I've explained all that." He smiled at Jamal and said, "Don't pay him any attention." Then he started to read Bethany's will.

" 'To my young friend, Jamal Jenkins—' "

"I can't believe this," Edward interrupted, rising to his feet.

"Edward," Jason said. "If you'll let me finish."

"I'm her only son."

"Yes, but—"

"Anything he gets"—he jerked his thumb in Jamal's direction—"I'll fight in court."

"Fine." Jason sighed. "Now, where was I? Ah, yes. 'To my young friend, Jamal Jenkins, I leave my most prized possession.' "

Edward slammed the table in anger. "That belongs to me! I've been robbed!"

Ignoring Edward, the lawyer now produced a small wooden box. He handed the box to the boy. Jamal held his breath. He imagined the box's contents—gold coins, thousand-dollar bills, diamonds.

Just then, the door opened slightly. Lenni, Alex, Tina, and Gaby were all peeking in. They had heard the shouting and couldn't resist.

"Open the box," barked Edward.

Jamal undid the tiny metal clasp and lifted the lid.

Inside was . . .

A battered old wooden chess set.

Edward burst into laughter. "Her most prized possession," he chortled. "That's rich."

"She also left you a note," Jason added. He handed Jamal a slip of paper with a chess problem on it and a three-by-five piece of paper with a typed message from Bethany:

Dear Jamal:
This doesn't seem like the biggest present, I know. You were hoping for money, right? But this is the best I can do in my special circumstances. And by taking it, you could do me a great favor. It's the only thing of real value I have left in the world. So please don't just throw it in the stove!

All right, it may not be your favorite gift, and it is a hand-me-down. But I want you to know that I had the great pleasure of beating my son with this set every time we played!

By the time you read this, you may have already grown tired of chess. Maybe you'd rather be out riding your bike or flying a kite! If so, please pass on this gift to someone who needs it more than you. But let me make this key Declaration to you. Chess is the best. There is no greater game.

Yours,

B. Franklin

P.S. Here's one last puzzle for you.
I know you won't rest until
you've solved it. (I hope I've
copied it correctly. These _bifocals_
of mine keep giving me trouble.)

your checkmate in three

Jamal stared at the note in disbelief. No diamonds, no gold coins, no riches. Just a rotten old chess set! A game he didn't even like!

"Well," Edward said with a big smile, "let's get on with it, Kohegan. What did *I* get?"

Edward took a seat as Jason Kohegan peered down at the will and read on. " 'Now, as for my son, Edward.' "

Edward clapped his hands together eagerly.

" 'I would like to remind you, Edward,' " the lawyer read, " 'that I have lent you money all my life. You gambled it all away. I simply can't give you any more. So with this will, I give you—not one red cent.' "

"What?!" Edward was back on his feet. He was yelling. "What about the ten thousand dollars?!"

"Maybe this will explain things better," said Mr. Kohegan. He handed Edward another typewritten note, on the same stationery as Jamal's. Edward read the note quickly, then threw it down in disgust. "I want my money!" he shouted.

As Edward argued with the lawyer, some of the letters on the note began to glow.

The adults couldn't see it. Only Jamal could. It cheered him up a great deal.

Because it was a sign that *he* was here! Ghostwriter!

2

"Hurry!"

"THIS IS AN OUTRAGE!" EDWARD YELLED. "I'm going to sue you and your entire law firm!"

The lawyer was trying to answer Edward, but Jamal wasn't listening. Lying near him on the table was that day's *New York Post*. And on the front page, the letters danced wildly as they rearranged themselves!

Jamal glanced at his friends, who were still staring in through the open doorway. When he looked back at the paper, the letters had stopped dancing. In their new order, the letters now spelled out a new message:

DEAR EDWARD, read the glowing headline. So, Ghostwriter had read Bethany's note to her son! And now he was showing the letter to Jamal.

As Edward and Mr. Kohegan continued to argue, Jamal carefully pulled the newspaper closer. Ghostwriter had changed the lead story into Bethany's note to Edward:

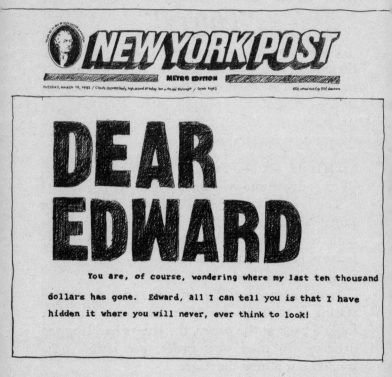

NEW YORK POST

METRO EDITION

TUESDAY, MARCH 10, 1992 / Cloudy, dryness likely, high around 40 today, low in the mid 30s tonight / Details Page 2

40¢ in New York City 50¢ elsewhere

DEAR EDWARD

You are, of course, wondering where my last ten thousand dollars has gone. Edward, all I can tell you is that I have hidden it where you will never, ever think to look!

"You are, of course, wondering where my last ten thousand dollars has gone. Edward, all I can tell you is that I have hidden it where you will never, ever think to look!"

Suddenly, a large hand grabbed the newspaper from Jamal. "Do you mind?" Edward said gruffly.

"Not at all," Jamal said.

Edward rolled up the paper and shoved it into the pocket of his overcoat. "The money is mine!" he warned the lawyer. Then he stalked out the door.

"Let's go to my house. We have to talk," Jamal said as soon as the five kids were outside.

Tina made a face. "I can't. I have to baby-sit my little sister," she said. "See you guys later."

"Later."

Jamal started to walk quickly toward home. Alex came up beside him. "Hey, Jamal, we saw Ghostwriter send you a message," he said in a low voice. "What did it say?"

"Later," Jamal repeated. And the group began to run.

By now, the kids were not surprised to get strange messages from the mysterious presence they called Ghostwriter. Not surprised, but very excited. They didn't know who Ghostwriter was, but they knew he was on their side.

They also knew that Ghostwriter was indeed

a ghost, a ghost who had died many years ago. And that he could communicate only through written words. He couldn't talk, or hear. But he could write, and he could read anything, anywhere.

One day, Ghostwriter had started writing to Jamal. Soon after that, he contacted Lenni, too. Next came Alex, then Gaby. And that was the start of the Ghostwriter team.

Back at the Jenkins house, Jamal flicked on the lights in his room and headed straight for his computer. His friends gathered around.

GHOSTWRITER, typed Jamal. WHAT'S GOING ON? WHERE DID BETHANY HIDE HER MONEY? AND WHAT AM I SUPPOSED TO DO ABOUT IT?

The screen was blank for a moment. Then the ghost's answer appeared on the monitor: I'M AFRAID I DON'T KNOW . . . DO YOU?

"What money?" Alex demanded.

Jamal told his friends about Bethany's letter to Edward. GHOSTWRITER, CAN YOU REMEMBER THE LETTER? he typed.

A moment later, the letter appeared on the computer screen. Lenni read it out loud. " 'I have hidden it where you will never, ever think to look,' " she finished. She looked at Jamal. "And you think maybe *you're* supposed to find this money?" she asked.

"I don't know. Bethany told me she had one

last puzzle for me," Jamal said. "I think I'm supposed to do *something*. But I don't know what."

"Bethany also said Edward was a gambler," Gaby said. She was pacing around Jamal's small room. "Maybe the money is in the bank. After all, gamblers aren't big on savings."

Alex gave his sister an annoyed look. "The lawyer said her bank account was empty, remember? And Edward made him show him the bank statement."

Jamal was busy typing in all his friends' ideas, so Ghostwriter could listen in on the meeting. Now he leaned back in his chair and flexed his fingers. "I don't know," he said. "Gaby may have something. Edward was obviously not a very good son, right? So what's a place a bad son doesn't go very often?"

"He doesn't go visit his mother," Lenni said.

Jamal gave Lenni a quick look. Her mother had died of cancer when she was only seven. "Good thinking," he told her, with extra enthusiasm.

He typed in her idea, but the screen remained blank.

"C'mon, Ghostwriter," Jamal whispered.

Gaby elbowed Alex to get a closer look at the screen.

"Hey," Alex said, "give me a break, would ya?"

Just then, words began to appear on the screen.

I THINK YOU'VE GOT SOMETHING, wrote the ghost.

The group whooped. Alex slapped Lenni on the back. "Okay," he said. "I guess this means we go to Bethany's apartment."

"I hope we're not too late," Jamal said, typing in his message as he spoke. "Are we?"

Ghostwriter answered immediately. But his message did not calm Jamal down. A single word appeared on the monitor.

HURRY!

The First Clue

"GOT IT !" LENNI WAS STARING INTO THE phone book. "Bethany Franklin. 259 Third Street."

"259," Gaby repeated, copying the address on her palm. Then she looked up. "That's twenty blocks. She *would* live far away."

"We'll just have to move it!" said Alex.

Jamal killed the lights, and the four friends raced into the kitchen.

"Stop!" Jamal's grandmother held up a hand to halt them. "Now, just where do you think you're going, my little millionaire?"

Jamal told her.

CeCe looked at the old chess set on the kitchen table and shook her head sadly. "I really thought you were going to hit the jackpot this time."

"I still might," Jamal replied, "but we've got to hurry."

CeCe laughed. "As my friend Stu Finkel always says, from your lips to God's ears."

The team banged out the front door and clattered down the steps. They ran so fast that the pens they wore around their necks—for writing to Ghostwriter—bounced around their ears.

They started walking again, after a block or so, then ran some more. When they finally got to Third Street, they were all pretty tired.

"Here it is." Alex read off the name on the mailbox. "Bethany Franklin. Apartment 3B."

"But how do we get in?" asked Gaby. She twisted the doorknob of the building's entrance door: it was locked.

"Maybe someone's home," Lenni said, buzzing the buzzer. They waited. No answer.

"Try the other buzzers," Gaby suggested. Jamal, Alex, and Lenni pushed all the buzzers, one after another. The intercom crackled. But when they tried to explain who they were, the intercom shut off again. They were back where they started.

"I've got it!" Gaby cried suddenly.

They all looked at her. She folded her arms and leaned her back against the door. "We'll just have to wait!"

"Brilliant," commented Alex sarcastically.

Just then, the door swung open. Gaby went flying backward. She almost fell but didn't.

But she had other things to worry about.

There was a Doberman pinscher snarling right in her face.

"Oh, don't worry," said an elderly Chinese man pulling on the dog's leash. "She's friendly. Sit, Brownie!" The dog sat.

Jamal explained that they were going up to Bethany Franklin's apartment.

"Ah," said the man. "My old neighbor. I miss her very much. I guess you're here to see her son."

The group exchanged glances.

"Edward?" Jamal asked.

"Yes, he was here an hour ago. I ran into him when he was leaving. He looked pretty angry, too. C'mon, Brownie!"

The dog bounded forward. Gaby ducked backward just in time as the Doberman hauled the short man out the door and down the front steps.

"Sounds like we're too late," Lenni said as they climbed the steps.

The door to 3B was slightly ajar. Alex knocked. Again, there was no answer.

"Edward?" Jamal called.

"I'm not going first," Gaby said. "With my luck, there's probably another dog in there."

Jamal wasn't taking any chances. He pushed open the door with his foot.

"Oh, no!" he gasped.

The tiny apartment had been totally torn apart. Sofa cushions were ripped open, their white stuffing leaking out onto the floor. Drawers had been dumped out. Chairs were upside down. Bethany's stuff littered the floor.

Jamal picked up a ripped sofa cushion and put it back on the sofa. "Nice to see that Edward is taking such good care of his mother's old stuff."

"If the money was here, I think we can figure that Edward already found it," said Alex.

Lenni bent down by an overturned bookcase. She picked up a few books, which were lying open and facedown. "Hey, look at this."

They gathered around her. The book was called *The World's 100 Best Chess Problems*. A bookmark was stuck in the middle, and the book fell open to that spot:

PROBLEM #43

"That's the problem Bethany gave me in her letter," Jamal said.

"Let me see the letter," Alex said. He held the two problems next to each other, and the group gathered around to compare.

"Yup," Alex agreed after a moment. "They're identical."

Mate in 2 moves

ATTENTION, READER! GO BACK TO PAGE 20, AND COMPARE THE TWO PROBLEMS. WHAT'S THE DIFFERENCE BETWEEN THE TWO?
—GHOSTWRITER

"Wait a minute!" Gaby said. "I see a difference."

Alex sighed. "Gaby, you don't always have to contradict me, you know. You can take my word for it once in a while."

Gaby gave her older brother a sympathetic look. "But they're different," she told him with a shrug.

"How?" Lenni asked.

Gaby pointed to the words at the bottom of the two problems. "In the book it says 'Mate in two.' That means you're supposed to be able to checkmate the other person in two moves. But when Bethany copied the problem for Jamal, she wrote 'Your checkmate in *three*.'"

"So she made a mistake," Alex said grumpily.

"I mean, her note says her bifocals were giving her trouble."

"Bifocals? You mean those glasses with the special lenses in the lower part?" Jamal picked up a pair of Bethany's glasses, which had been knocked to the floor along with everything else. The lenses were cracked now, but they were regular glasses, not bifocals at all.

"She always seemed like a really sharp lady," he remembered. "And she said she had one last puzzle for me. What if *this* is the puzzle? What if it's some kind of a clue?"

"Ghostwriter thinks we're on to something!" cried Lenni, who had been scribbling in her notebook. As the group watched, Ghostwriter used the letters Lenni had already written to assemble a message: YES . . . A CLUE.

"A clue?" Alex moved around the room, trying to avoid stepping on anything. "'Your checkmate in three?'" He scratched his head. "Could 'three' refer to a place where the money is hidden?"

"Three," mused Jamal. "I don't know."

"Or maybe it means we have to move three things in this place in order to find the secret safe," Gaby suggested. She peeked behind the old pictures hanging on the walls. The pictures were framed watercolors signed by Bethany. There was nothing behind them but peeling wallpaper.

"What if it means 'Your check, mate...'" Lenni offered. "You know, like she's trying to tell us she wrote Jamal a check."

"But her bank account was empty," Jamal pointed out. "And that still doesn't explain the 'in three' part."

"I'm stumped," Gaby sighed. She sat down on top of Bethany's strange old wood-burning stove.

"Me, too," agreed Lenni. She looked around the wrecked apartment. "You know, maybe we should rearrange everything around here before we go. I feel bad for poor Bethany if we leave the place like this."

"Rearrange?" repeated Jamal, lost in thought. Then he grabbed Lenni's notebook. MAYBE BETHANY MEANT FOR US TO REAR-RANGE THE LETTERS! he wrote.

"What is it?" Alex asked him.

"I had an idea," said Jamal. "Maybe the clue is one of those... one of those... I forget what you call them. Where you rearrange the letters."

"Oh, yeah," Alex said. "They're called—"

"Anagrams," chimed in Gaby.

Alex grinned at her. "That's just what I was going to say."

There was a pause as they watched Lenni's notebook. Then the letters she had written began to rearrange themselves. Next to a jumble of left-over letters, Ghostwriter wrote, YES! ANA-GRAM.

"All right!" exclaimed Lenni.

"Let's get to work," Jamal said. Lenni ripped out pages of her notebook and handed them around. Then she ripped out an extra page. At the top she wrote, YOUR CHECKMATE IN THREE. GO, GHOSTWRITER!

Immediately, the letters came to life, swirling around the page. CHARM, Ghostwriter wrote. METER. MATCH. ITCH. HAM. HARM.

Lenni slipped off her neck pen and uncapped it. She stared at the letters in the words before her. Where to begin? She wrote down an *h*, then an *i*. Was there also an *n* and a *t*? Yes! "Hint," she called out.

"That sounds good," Alex said. "I mean, a clue is a kind of a hint."

Lenni crossed out the letters from *hint* and tried to play around with the remaining letters, to see if she could make them into words. But she got stuck.

"Mike in theater," called out Jamal.

"Real anagrams use *all* the letters," Gaby said, looking over his shoulder.

"All right. What do you have, since you're so smart?"

Gaby looked at her page. "Nothing any better."

Alex studied his sheet. "Me, neither. What about Ghostwriter?"

Gaby held up the page, which was covered

with phrases front and back. "Just a lot of words that don't make much sense."

Jamal looked out the grimy window. On the street below, an old man trudged past Bethany's building. "Maybe we're wasting our time," he said. "Maybe it's not an anagram at all."

"I'm getting writer's cramp," Alex complained, shaking out his fingers.

"Should we stop?" Gaby said.

Jamal glanced at Alex. "You make the call," Alex said.

They all looked at Lenni, who was the only one still writing. "You make the . . ." she echoed. "Hey! That works."

They quickly gathered around her. "Let me see," she said. "If the message starts with 'You make the,' then that would leave . . ." She crossed out the letters from you make the and wrote out the remaining letters.

YOU MAKE THE . . . CNRTEERHCI

"That looks too long for one word," Alex said. "Maybe split it in two."

Lenni scribbled quickly:

YOU MAKE THE . . . CNRTEE RHCI

Alex was squeezing his head between Jamal's shoulder and Gaby's head to get a look at Lenni's pad.

That meant that when he screamed, he screamed right in his younger sister's ear.

"I see it!"

4

Rally!—A

"YOU MAKE THE CENTER RICH!" ALEX yelled.

The friends stared at each other in amazement.

"So Bethany *does* want you to find the money, Jamal," Lenni whispered.

"And give it to the community center," whispered Gaby.

"It's a treasure hunt," whispered Alex.

"Her last puzzle," whispered Gaby.

"Why are we all whispering?" Jamal asked.

But he was whispering, too. He looked around the tiny apartment. He suddenly had the creepy feeling that someone was eavesdropping on their meeting.

"Why didn't she just leave the money to the

center in her will?" Alex said, puzzled.

"Because she knew Edward would fight the will," replied Lenni. She was remembering the threats Edward made in the lawyer's office.

"Wait a second," Jamal said. He tiptoed toward the front door. Then he yanked it open.

There was no one there. He breathed a sigh of relief.

"Okay," Alex said quietly. "So where do we go from here?"

The kids exchanged blank glances. No one had an answer. Lenni looked down at her notebook. Ghostwriter was silent, too.

"Well," she offered, "there's one bit of good news."

"What's that?" Jamal asked.

"Bethany's neighbor said that Edward looked pretty angry when he left here."

Jamal shrugged. "So?"

"So, that means he hasn't found Bethany's treasure, either!"

"Now, let's say the man has only half a tank of gas, how many miles across the desert will his car travel?"

As Ms. Meecham droned on, Alex ducked his head down and finished folding his note. He waited until Ms. Meecham turned back to the chalkboard. Then he passed the note to the girl who sat next to him. "For Janet Williams," he mouthed.

She gave him a big smile. Girls liked Alex. Then she turned and slid the note onto Janet's desk. It caught on the wire of her spiral-bound notebook, and there was a loud tearing noise.

Ms. Meecham turned back with a puzzled look on her face. She stared at the class suspiciously. Then she continued, "Let's call the amount of gas in the tank *G,* and the number of miles the car travels *M.*"

Janet picked up the note and looked around the room. Then she spotted Alex, who was motioning for her to open it. She hid the note under her desk and started to read.

Alex had written: "Here's a weird story for you. It involves someone you knew."

The note went on to tell Janet the story of the team's hunt for Bethany Franklin's treasure. Alex remembered seeing Janet at the community center once or twice with Bethany. Maybe, since Janet had known Bethany, she could tell him something useful.

The one thing Alex left out of the note was Ghostwriter. Janet was nice, but she wasn't on the team. No one outside the team could know about Ghostwriter.

When Janet finished reading the note she looked over at Alex and made a soundless whistle.

Then she tore out a piece of notebook paper, ripping one hole at a time so Ms. Meecham wouldn't catch her. She began writing furiously.

Could Janet know something? Alex was staring at her with excitement when Ms. Meecham repeated her question for the third time.

"I *said*," Ms. Meecham said, "what answer did you get, Alex?"

"Uh, um, ah," Alex stammered.

Ms. Meecham held out a piece of red chalk. "Right this way, sir."

Ms. Meecham ended up keeping Alex after school. He had to write "I will pay attention in class" a hundred times. As soon as he was done, he pocketed what was left of the chalk and hurried out to the schoolyard. He knelt down.

RALLY!—A he wrote carefully.

A faint glow shimmered around the letters, then vanished. Alex smiled. Ghostwriter was already at work!

Moments later, Jamal was walking past a newsstand when the headlines on the papers rearranged and flashed bright yellow: RALLY!—A.

Home alone, Lenni had just heated up a can of alphabet soup. She was about to stir the steaming soup with her spoon when the noodle letters began to swim around in a rapid circle. They floated across the surface of the soup in a new order: RALLY!—A.

At the same moment, Mrs. Fernandez was asking Gaby, "Could you mail this for me on your way to the park?" She handed the letter to her daughter as Gaby headed out the door.

The letters on the envelope's address were glowing bright yellow: RALLY!—A.

But Gaby didn't look at the letter. She dropped it into the mailbox on the corner.

Then she started bouncing her tiny Super Ball down the busy Brooklyn street. She bounced it past the movie theater, where the marquee now read, RALLY!—A. She dribbled past the wall where the graffiti spray paint swirled into a new pattern: RALLY!—A. Without looking, she crumpled the wrapper on the candy bar she bought at the corner store: RALLY!—A.

Finally, she stood at the corner, waiting to cross the busy street. She bounced her ball impatiently, waiting for the light to change. The wait seemed endless. She stared across the street at the red Don't Walk sign.

Except it didn't say Don't Walk anymore. It flashed, TALK NOW!

Then that message disappeared, as the light now flashed, A!

Gaby pocketed the tiny ball, turned, and ran.

"Sorry I'm late," she gasped as she raced into her brother's room ten minutes later. She was the last one there.

"It's okay," Alex said. He was sitting on the edge of his bed. "Here's what I've got. Janet

Williams knew Bethany. They took a creative writing class together at the community center. She says Bethany hardly ever wrote about anything but the Revolutionary War."

The group stared at him blankly.

"She was an American history buff," he added.

"So? Where does that get us?" Jamal asked.

"Who knows?" Alex said. "But it's a start. After this meeting, I'm going to go to the library and start reading up on American history. Who wants to help?"

He looked at Lenni, who grimaced. She preferred to read about music than American history any day. "I don't know, I'm kind of busy with a lot of—"

Alex grinned. "Good. You just volunteered."

"I'm going to call that lawyer Kohegan and tell him what's been going on," Jamal said.

They looked at Gaby. "I'll go to the community center and talk to Mrs. Ward, the center's director," she said. "Bethany used to hang out there a lot, so maybe she can tell us something else important about her."

"Good thinking," Jamal said. "Why don't we all meet there in about . . ." He looked at the wall clock. "Two hours?"

Two hours later, Jamal walked into the community center and headed for room B3—the chess club. He found Alex bent over a board, playing against an older boy. Lenni was sitting nearby, watching. Alex moved his queen as Jamal approached. "Checkmate," he said with a grin.

His opponent scowled. Mr. Santana came by and marked down Alex's name on his clipboard.

"Nice going, Alex," said Mr. Santana. "That means you'll be representing the center in tomorrow's all-Brooklyn tournament!"

"Cool!" Jamal congratulated him.

"Way to go, Alex," said Lenni.

Alex shrugged and stood up. "I couldn't have beaten Bethany."

"Speaking of Bethany . . ." Jamal was carrying Bethany's old chess set. "I figure you guys could use this set more than I can," he said. He unlatched the box and dumped the pieces into the large bucket of chess pieces Mr. Santana had set up on one of the desks.

"How did it go at the library?" he asked Alex and Lenni.

"Great," said Alex.

"Horrible," said Lenni. "Look!"

There were two stacks of library books about American history piled on another desk. "Alex expects me to read one of those piles."

"What's wrong with that?" Jamal asked with a smile.

"Just looking at them gives me a headache."

Behind them, Mr. Santana was erasing his

notes from the chalkboard. Transportation to the Tournament Should Be Arranged, read one line, but when he was done, he had wiped away everything except for the last part of the word Arranged.

The supervisor paused by the light switch. "You kids going to play some more chess?"

"No," Alex said, "but we want to stick around for a few minutes, if that's okay."

"Sure, but don't stay too long. The center is closing soon." He gave Alex a thumbs-up gesture. "I'll see *you* at the tournament."

Mr. Santana bumped into Gaby on his way out. She was running.

"Whoops! Sorry!" she said.

"You're too late," he teased as he left. "The tournament's over."

"Listen to this," Gaby told the group. "Mrs. Ward remembers Bethany very well. When I told her about our hunch, that Bethany wanted to give her money to the center, she said the center is really short on cash. She says if they don't get more money soon, they'll have to start a new schedule, and only stay open half the week."

"That's terrible," said Lenni.

"I know." Gaby looked at Alex. "The chess club would be canceled."

"No!"

Gaby turned to Jamal. "And the video game room would be closed."

Jamal groaned. "Now, *that's* bad."

"There's more. She says that Bethany knew the center needed money. Mrs. Ward told her. And guess how much money they need to stay open full-time?"

"Ten thousand dollars?" breathed Lenni.

"Exactly."

Alex snapped his fingers. "Bethany spent a lot of time here. But I never saw Edward here, did you?"

"No," agreed Lenni. "And it's a good thing, too. That guy gave me the creeps."

"'I have hidden it where you will never, ever think to look,'" Alex quoted Bethany.

"The center!" Gaby said, her eyes wide.

"I'll take the basement," Lenni said, heading for the door.

They fanned out, searching every room. Twenty minutes later, they were back in the chess room, wearing dusty, disappointed faces.

"Well, that's it," Jamal concluded. "We've searched everywhere."

"Except here." Alex gestured around the room. His glance fell on the chalkboard. On the letters that Mr. Santana had missed when he wiped the board clean: RANGED.

Only now the letters were moving.

"Look!" said Alex.

Ghostwriter had rearranged the letters into a new word: DANGER.

Then the lights flicked out.

A Surprise
Visit

FOR AN INSTANT, NONE OF THE KIDS MOVED
or spoke. Then they heard the sound of footsteps,
coming closer down the hall. And closer.

"Run!" cried Alex.

The four kids stumbled out of the dark room.
Into the dark hallway. At the end of the dark
hallway stood a large, stocky man, about six feet
tall. All they could see was his outline—his face
was in shadow. He was holding a rifle.

"Edward!" hissed Jamal.

The kids turned and raced in the other direction.

"Hey! Stop!" the man yelled.

Jamal crashed into the double doors at the end
of the hallway. The doors didn't open. "Oh,

man," he moaned, clutching his shoulder in pain.

The man was running down the hallway toward them.

"This way!" cried Lenni. She pulled Jamal by his good arm as the foursome headed out the emergency exit. The alarm sounded. They raced up the stairs two at a time.

The front hallway was pitch-black. They groped toward the front door. Suddenly, Alex felt his arms close around someone huge and hairy. He screamed as the figure wrestled him to the ground with a horrible crash.

Then the lights blazed on. Alex found himself lying on the ground, his arms wrapped around an overcoat and a wooden coat tree.

Gaby helped him to his feet as Jamal hurried to the front door. "C'mon," he urged.

Then he turned the knob. They were locked in!

"Split up," Alex commanded. But just then, the door to the stairway opened.

And the tall man was blocking their way.

He pointed the rifle.

Except it wasn't a rifle at all.

It was a mop.

"Just what do you kids think you're doing?" the man growled. It was Louis, the community center's custodian.

Louis was breathing heavily. Now he took out

a handkerchief and mopped his brow. "Boy, did you give me a scare! What's the matter with you, playing a trick on me like that? I thought you were burglars!"

"Gave *you* a scare!" Gaby gasped. Then she looked at Alex, and she started to laugh. "I think your coat attacked my brother."

"Very funny," Alex said, but he was grinning, too.

"I nearly broke my arm," said Jamal, rubbing his shoulder. But he joined in the laughter, too.

He was still laughing when he told his grandmother the story later that night.

"I was so sure it was Edward Franklin, I can't tell you."

CeCe chuckled. "I think you're letting your imagination get a little carried away." She turned and headed for her bedroom. "If you hear a strange knock at our front door tonight, don't answer. It might be the custodian from the community center!" She was still laughing as she closed her bedroom door.

Jamal laughed, too. Then he heard a strange knock at the front door.

He froze. Was he imagining things?

Knock-knock-knock. Louder now. And very real.

Jamal looked through the peephole. He saw a large, angry face with a gray-and-black mustache.

The face was distorted by the peephole's fisheye lens. But he could still recognize it.

Edward Franklin.

Edward knocked again. And Jamal's dad strode into the living room. "What's going on?"

"It's—ah—" Jamal stammered.

"Who's there?" his dad demanded.

Jamal stammered some more.

Mr. Jenkins yanked the door open. He stared at Edward.

"Mr. Jenkins?" Edward asked, with a smile. "Hi, Jamal."

"You know this man?" Mr. Jenkins asked his son. Jamal nodded.

Edward's oily smile broadened. "I'm sorry to trouble you, but I'm here to offer your boy some money. I figured you wouldn't mind that."

"Money?" Mr. Jenkins frowned. "For what?" But he stood aside and let Edward enter.

Edward looked around the living room. "Nice place," he remarked, grinning.

"Now, what's this about money?" Mr. Jenkins said.

"Well, I assume Jamal told you about my mother, Bethany."

"Oh, yes." Mr. Jenkins looked surprised. "But I thought that was all settled."

"Oh, it is, it is," Edward assured him. "It's just that, well, you see, in her will, my mother left Jamal an old chess set."

He was looking around the room. Was he looking for the chess set? Jamal crossed his arms.

"The thing is," Edward went on, "I've been playing a lot of chess lately. Do you mind if I sit down?" Mr. Jenkins nodded, and the big man sat on the sofa. He didn't look much shorter, even when he was sitting! "I know she left the set to you, Jamal, but you see, it has a great sentimental value for me."

What was Edward driving at? Why was he so interested in the chess set all of a sudden?

"I'd be willing to buy it from you."

"It's not for sale," Jamal said quickly. He wasn't sure why he said it.

Edward smiled at him. "Well," he said. He leaned forward. At first, Jamal thought he was going to get up. But instead, he reached in his back pocket and pulled out a thick, dark leather wallet. "That's a shame. Because I'd be willing to make it worth your while." He opened the wallet and counted out three twenty-dollar bills. He laid them side by side on the coffee table.

Sixty dollars! Jamal didn't know much about chess, but he was sure that that set wasn't worth more than five dollars, used and battered as it was. Why would—? Suddenly Jamal had it. Why hadn't he thought of it before? The treasure! It must be hidden inside one of the pieces!

A picture flashed through Jamal's mind. He saw himself at the community center, dumping the chess pieces into the large bucket of pieces.

Edward was staring at him with gleaming eyes. "Do we have a deal?"

"No," said Jamal. "Sorry."

Edward started to rise, his smile suddenly turning into a threatening leer.

Mr. Jenkins draped an arm over his son's shoulder. "You heard what he said. No deal."

Edward laughed. It wasn't a nice laugh. "I guess that chess set must be pretty special to you, too, huh?" He peered at Jamal closely. "Any particular reason you like it so much?"

When Jamal didn't answer, Mr. Jenkins said, "He needs it for tomorrow's tournament. Right, son?"

"Right."

Edward laughed again. Then he reached back into the wallet. He took out another bill and laid it next to the other ones. Except this bill was a hundred. He looked at Jamal.

"No deal," Jamal repeated.

The next day, Jamal skipped breakfast and raced to the center. After making sure he wasn't being followed, he went straight to room B3. The lights were off. The bucket of chess pieces sat on one of the desks.

Except the bucket was empty.

"Oh, hi, Jamal."

Jamal's head jerked up. Mr. Santana stood in

the doorway.

"Where are the pieces?" Jamal said, breath-lessly.

"What's that?"

"The pieces. The chess pieces."

"Jamal, don't tell me you've finally given up the world of video games." Mr. Santana smiled. "I brought our chess sets over to the high school for the tournament. They're expecting quite a turnout, and they need every piece they can get."

"But I dumped my set in here, and now I need to get it back. The pieces have a red dot on the back of them and—"

"You're welcome to take them back," Mr. Santana assured him. "But they're going to be locked up until this afternoon. If you want to come by then—"

But Jamal was already running out of the room. He used the pay phone next to Anne Ward's office. He pulled out the wrinkled business card he had been carrying in his back pocket: Jason Kohegan, Lawyer/Abogado.

"Mr. Kohegan? This is Jamal Jenkins."

"Yes. Call me Jason."

"I'm sorry to bother you, but—"

"That's fine. I told you, anytime. Is everything okay?"

"Well, Edward Franklin came by my apartment last night."

The lawyer sighed. "At your home? That guy

is something else. What did he want?"

"He wanted to buy my chess set."

"Your chess set?"

"I know. I couldn't figure it out, either. But then it hit me. The missing money. I bet it's hidden in one of the pieces."

"Oh, dear," Mr. Kohegan said with a chuckle. "This is really turning into a treasure hunt, isn't it? And have you checked the chess set?"

"That's the thing—I can't. The pieces are being used in this afternoon's all-Brooklyn chess tournament. I won't be able to check them until then."

"Oh, dear," Mr. Kohegan said again. "All right. Let me write down the information, and I'll meet you at the tournament."

"Thank you!" said Jamal. He was feeling better already. "Um, should I also call the police?"

"No. No need to," Mr. Kohegan assured him. "I'll handle it all myself."

6

Playing for Keeps

"SPECTATOR OR PLAYER?" ASKED A woman with a clipboard.

"Spectator," Jamal said.

"Player," said Alex, giving his name.

Then they hurried into the gym. "I hope they haven't put out the pieces yet," Jamal said.

"Don't worry," Alex said. "How hard can it be to find pieces with a red—"

He stopped in midsentence. They had turned the corner into a vast gymnasium filled with row after row of card tables. There were even tables on the stage. A long white sign stretched from wall to wall, reading, Welcome, Brooklyn Chess Fans! Beneath the banner, hundreds of chess players were locked in combat over eight-by-eight boards. Countless spectators moved quietly between the rows, studying the positions. And laid out on the tables were thousands of chess pieces.

"We're sunk," moaned Jamal.

A hand clapped Jamal on the shoulder.

"Mr. Kohegan," Jamal said with a grin of relief.

The small man wiped his forehead with a hanky. "Whew," he said. "Looks like we've got our work cut out for us."

"I'll check all the pieces in the games I play," Alex promised.

"Look!" Jamal pointed to a table in the last row.

A tall, angry man with a mustache was playing chess against a twelve-year-old girl. The man seemed to be studying the pieces that had been taken *off* the board, instead of the pieces in the game itself.

"Edward," said Jamal.

"Alex!" Mr. Santana was waving at Alex.

"See ya," Alex said as he headed off.

"I'll take the first row, you take the second," Mr. Kohegan told Jamal.

"Deal."

He stood behind the first player he came to, a thirteen-year-old Korean boy he recognized from school. He craned his neck, looking for pieces with the red dot.

"Do you mind?" the boy asked, looking up at him.

Jamal moved on. He had made it past seven tables when he bumped into another spectator, Tina Nguyen.

"I thought you didn't like chess," she said with a smile.

"Tina! Do me a favor, would ya?" He whispered his instructions in her ear, then he moved to the other side of the row to check the backs of the other pieces.

"Hopeless," he kept telling himself. "This is hopeless."

Then he saw it.

The player in front of him—a big, burly redheaded man—had a black pawn with a red dot.

There was only one little problem.

It was still on the board.

The man turned and stared at Jamal. He smiled back. The man scowled. Then he turned back to the board. The pawn with the red dot was facing off against a white pawn. If the man traded pawns, the red-dot pawn would be off the board.

The man lifted the red-dot pawn, about to move it. His opponent smiled at him, as if to say, "What a bad move!"

The redheaded man put the pawn back down.

"No!" Jamal said aloud.

The man stared at him in amazement.

"Sorry," Jamal said. He tried to grin.

"You think I should trade pawns?" the man asked him.

"Hey, you're not allowed to get help," his opponent complained.

Jamal nodded at the man. And the man traded pawns.

Jamal immediately picked up the red-dot pawn. He peeled back the piece's felt bottom to see if there was anything inside. It was hollow.

"Bad move," the man's opponent was saying. Jamal looked back at the board. "I was dying for you to make that trade. Check."

The redheaded man threw Jamal a furious look. "Sorry," Jamal whispered. He moved on to the next table.

Twenty minutes later, he had checked two more rows. Alex came over to him. "I won," he said with a smile. "But no red-dot pieces."

"Keep looking."

"I will," he promised as he headed off to his next game.

Fifty minutes later, Jamal had checked ten red-dot pieces. Tina had checked six. Kohegan had checked eleven. "That leaves five pieces," Jamal said.

"Two pieces," Alex corrected. "My last opponent had three red-dot pieces. I got so distracted, I lost the game."

"Well, if we find the treasure, it'll all be worth it," said Jamal.

"I'm afraid we've checked every row," Mr. Kohegan said. "Are you sure Bethany left you a complete set?"

"Positive," replied Jamal. "At least, I think so."

";Great," said Alex.

At a nearby table, two players were just sitting down to play. One of the players was Edward.

"Director," Edward called. "We need pieces."

One of the tournament aides went behind the stage and brought out a new bucket.

"Let's go," Alex said.

7

A Hidden Message

"HERE YOU GO, GENTLEMEN," THE TOUR-
nament aide said to Edward and his opponent.
She handed over the large bucket of pieces.

Edward grabbed it out of her hand and dumped
it out on the table.

There lay the two missing red-dot pieces: the
white queen and the black rook. Jamal reached
over and snatched up the queen.

"Hey," said the chess player who was going
to be playing white.

Jamal peeled back the felt. Nothing.

"Sorry," he apologized, handing back the
queen.

They were all watching Edward now. He had
the black rook in his hand. He stood up from

the table, backing away from them.

"Let's see that piece," Alex demanded.

"Where are you going?" Edward's opponent asked.

"We'll call the police if we have to," Jason Kohegan warned.

Edward peeled back the rook's felt bottom.

He looked inside.

"There's something there!" Jamal said eagerly.

With two trembling fingers, Edward pulled out—

A blank piece of paper.

With some holes cut out of it.

"Garbage!" Edward shouted. He stared at the paper for a moment, then tossed it down on the chessboard in utter disgust.

"I don't understand," Jamal said, looking at the paper.

"Don't you see?" Edward told him. "There never was any money. This was all just my mother's idea of a joke."

Edward's opponent was staring up at him in amazement. "Are you going to play, or what?"

Edward waved a hand at him as he walked away. "I give up," he said.

"You forfeit?"

"Right." He pointed at Jamal. "You hear me? I give up."

"Director!" called Edward's opponent. "We have a forfeit."

Jason picked up the blank piece of paper. He held it up to the light. He handed it to Jamal. "I'm afraid Edward is right," he said. "I think this was all just a wild-goose chase."

GHOSTWRITER, typed Jamal. WE'RE STUCK.

The screen was blank. Then: SO AM <u>I</u>.

"No," moaned Gaby. She grabbed a handful of the popcorn Mrs. Jenkins had made for the group and crammed it into her mouth.

It was the day after the tournament. Jamal had called a rally to update everyone about the tournament and Bethany's chess set.

Jamal was staring at the screen. He moved the blinking cursor right under Ghostwriter's underlined word.

TELL ME SOMETHING, he typed. WHY DID YOU UNDERLINE THIS WORD?

UNDERLINED WORDS ARE IMPORTANT WORDS THAT THE AUTHOR WANTS TO STRESS.

SO, WHAT ABOUT THE WORDS BETHANY UNDERLINED IN HER NOTE?

Ghostwriter paused.

"Good thinking," said Lenni.

GOOD THINKING, typed Ghostwriter.

"See?" Lenni smiled. "Great minds think alike."

Alex said, "Let's look at that note again."

Jamal opened his desk drawer and pulled out three video game disks, a paperback of video game tips, and a half-eaten brownie.

"Don't tell me you lost the note," Gaby said.

"Gaby," Jamal replied, "don't be silly. I didn't lose the note."

He pulled out a penknife, a yo-yo, an empty Silly Putty egg, a plastic protractor, a wooden ruler, a pair of big plastic-nose glasses, a pair of scissors, and a leaky pen.

"I lost her note," he said.

"Well, then, I think we're really sunk," Alex said. He started playing with the yo-yo, making it sleep.

Lenni put on the plastic-nose glasses. "At least you found my gag glasses," she told him. "These are worth almost a dollar."

Jamal was staring at his empty desk drawer. "Aha!" he cried. He pulled out a letter that had been tucked into the back of the drawer. Alex grabbed it out of his hand.

"Dear, Jamal," he read. "I don't want to rub it in. But college is so cool."

"That's from my sister Danitra," Jamal explained with a sigh.

He slammed his desk drawer shut.

"How do I look in these things?" Lenni asked, moving to the mirror.

On the computer screen, Ghostwriter typed,

WHAT SEEMS TO BE THE PROBLEM?

Jamal was about to answer when Lenni started to laugh.

"Lenni," Alex said, "they don't look *that* funny."

But Lenni just kept laughing. She was pointing, too. What she was pointing at was the piece of paper that Jamal had tucked into the corner of the mirror's frame. It was Bethany's note.

They gathered around it, looking at the underlined words.

"Stove," Alex said. "Why would she want to stress the word *stove*?"

"What about that funny-looking old stove in Bethany's apartment?" asked Gaby. "Did we check it?"

"We had to," Jamal said. "We checked every inch of that place."

"But did we check *in* the stove?" Lenni asked.

"I remember I sat on it," Gaby said. "But I don't think I—"

Jamal had already picked up the phone and was dialing. "Mr. Kohegan, please," he said. "It's Jamal Jenkins."

He covered the mouthpiece with his hand as he explained to the group, "He can get us back in to Bethany's apartment."

"Oh, wow! It's in the stove," Gaby cried. "I know it! I know it!"

"Gaby," Alex said. "Calm down." He tossed

the yo-yo down hard. The string broke, and the toy rolled under the radiator.

When Jason Kohegan heard what was going on, he said, "Oh, dear. I'm afraid Edward cleaned out the apartment long ago. He sold everything to a junk dealer. I don't think he got much for it, though. Why? Was there something you wanted?"

Jamal explained about the stove.

Jason laughed. "You guys don't give up very easily, do you? I like that." There was a pause. "No," he continued, "I just can't remember which junk dealer Edward hired. I could call Edward and ask—but that might make him suspicious."

"No, don't do that," Jamal said, rubbing his head. "Maybe we can find him. Thanks."

Jamal hung up. He shook his head. "No way."

"But the treasure is in the stove," Gaby shrieked. "I'm sure of it!"

"What makes you so sure?" Jamal said.

"I've got a hunch."

Jamal started typing, filling Ghostwriter in on what had been going on. IS THE STOVE WORTH CHECKING?

I DOUBT IT.

Jamal looked at Gaby. She crossed her arms tightly over her chest. "You guys never listen to me. The money is in the stove, okay?"

"Where are you going?" Lenni asked her.

"I'm going over to Tina's house." Gaby shouldered her backpack. "If you don't want to search for the junk dealer, Tina will."

"Well," Jamal said, "maybe it's a good idea for us to split up the chores. Gaby, you try to track down that dealer. And we'll—"

"We'll what?" Alex said.

"We'll talk to Ghostwriter and try to come up with more clues," Jamal said helplessly.

He typed the decision into the computer, adding, SOUND GOOD?

Ghostwriter didn't answer.

Tina's family lived in back of her father's tailor shop on the corner of River Street and Fourth Avenue. Gaby bought an apple at the market next door, then went into the shop. "Is Tina home?" she asked Mr. Nguyen, who was hunched over a sewing machine.

He smiled. "Hi, Gaby. Go on in."

She found Tina sitting at her desk, writing in her log book. The ten-year-old glanced up, smiled, then kept working. "Just a sec."

"What are you doing?"

"I said just a sec." She finished writing. "Logging in some new shots for my Monday *Action News* spot." Tina was the producer of her school's news video. She closed the notebook. "Okay," she said. "What's up?"

She steepled her hands under her chin as Gaby

told her what was going on. Gaby was waving her arms excitedly. Tina remained calm. "The problem is," Gaby concluded, "we can't ask Edward what junk dealer he used. So how will we ever know? I mean, it's not like we know any junk dealers we can ask."

"No," Tina said. "But we've got a special reference book that could help us."

"We do? What?"

"I'll give you a hint. It's yellow."

"The Yellow Pages!" Gaby slapped her forehead. "Why didn't I think of that?"

"Now," said Tina, "the only problem is, where is it?"

It was a ten-minute search before they found the Yellow Pages. (Tina's mother was using the phone book as a doorstop.) Gaby grabbed the book. "What do we look under?"

"Let's try 'Junk.'"

Gaby turned to the letter *J*. Then she slammed the book shut. "It's not here. It goes right from 'Jewelry Repair' to 'Karate Lessons.'"

"Are you sure?" Tina reopened the book to the letter *J*. "'Jewelry Repair,'" she read, moving her index finger slowly down the page. "'Jewels—Imitation Stones, Juices . . .'" Her forefinger halted. "'Junk D-l-r-s.'"

"It *is* there!"

"What's D-l-r-s?" Tina wondered.

"D-l-r-s is an abbreviation for *dealers*," said

Gaby. "All right! Now we're getting some-where." She peered at the spot marked by her friend's finger and let out a moan. "Oh, no. Look at how many there are. We'll never be able to check all those."

"Don't worry," Tina said. "We'll let our fingers do the walking. C'mon."

Tina's brother Tuan was on the kitchen phone. He waved angrily when Tina tapped him on the shoulder.

They waited five minutes, but Tuan was still showing no signs of getting off the phone.

Glaring at her brother one last time, Tina led Gaby back to her room. "Okay, I've got a new plan. Step one," she said, ripping a piece of paper out of her notebook. Then she carefully copied over the list of junk dealer phone numbers. She handed Gaby the list. She emptied out her piggy bank, and handed Gaby half the quarters that she had spilled out onto her bed. "Let's go," she said, picking up the phone book. Then she led Gaby out to a row of pay phones on the corner.

"You start from the bottom of your list," Tina told Gaby. "I'll start from the top of mine."

"Will you take those things off already?" Jamal said. "You look like Groucho Marx."

Lenni was still wearing the plastic glasses with the big nose and black mustache. She stooped over and did a Groucho Marx walk around the room. In her best Groucho voice, she said, "Like Groucho? Why, that's the most ridiculous thing I've ever heard."

But she took off the glasses. "Let's face it," she said. "We're stumped. Maybe we should take a break."

NO, answered Ghostwriter, when Jamal typed in her suggestion.

SO WHAT SHOULD WE DO?

PLEASE GIVE ME A LIST OF ALL THE EVIDENCE AND CLUES YOU HAVE SO FAR.

Jamal sighed. "That's going to be a short list."

"Here, I'll type," Alex offered. He took Jamal's place at the computer.

ONE CHESS SET. PIECES HAVE RED DOT ON BACK. INSIDE ONE PIECE WAS SOME PAPER.

"BE SPECIFIC," Ghostwriter urged.

"How can I be more specific than that?" Alex asked his friends.

"Let's see," said Lenni. "Say which piece had the paper inside."

Alex deleted ONE PIECE and typed in: THE BLACK ROOK.

"Do we still have the paper?" Lenni asked Jamal.

Jamal pulled it out of his pocket. Lenni measured it with Jamal's ruler.

"Lenni," Jamal said, "I don't see how this is

going to get us anywhere."

"I know," Lenni agreed. "That's because we don't really know what we're looking for yet. So, any clue might help, right?" She finished measuring. "Five by three inches," she told Alex. "With six holes in it."

He typed in this info. Then he continued his list. BETHANY'S NOTE TO EDWARD. WHICH YOU HAVE ALREADY READ. He thought for a moment.

"What Janet told you," Jamal prompted.

WE KNOW THAT BETHANY WAS AN AMERICAN HISTORY BUFF.

AND SHE WROTE POETRY, Ghostwriter added.

WE KNOW THE CENTER NEEDS TEN THOUSAND DOLLARS, Alex continued with his list. AND THAT BETHANY WANTS JAMAL TO MAKE THE CENTER RICH. AND WE KNOW THAT BETHANY UNDERLINED THE WORD *STOVE* FOR SOME REASON. GABY AND TINA ARE CHECKING ON THAT.

He stared at the screen. THAT'S IT, he typed.

WHAT ABOUT BETHANY'S NOTE TO JAMAL? wrote Ghostwriter.

"Five by three inches," Lenni answered, measuring it. Alex typed it in.

They all stared at the screen. Then Lenni said,

"Okay, Jamal, you were right. It was a waste of time."

ATTENTION, READER!
STUDY THE LIST OF EVIDENCE CLOSELY
DO YOU SEE A NEW CLUE?
WHAT TWO PIECES OF EVIDENCE MATCH?
—GHOSTWRITER

"Maybe it was a waste of time, but maybe it wasn't," Jamal said. He was still staring at the screen. "Look."

Ghostwriter was typing a new message. FIVE BY THREE, FIVE BY THREE. THE TWO PIECES OF PAPER ARE THE SAME SIZE.

"So what?" Jamal said aloud.

"So maybe they're the same size for a reason,"

Alex said.

Lenni was holding up the blank piece of paper. "I probably just measured wrong." She put it down over Bethany's note. And turned it. It fit perfectly.

"Oh, wow," she said, looking down. She let out a scream. "There it is!"

Bethany's hidden message was now clear.

ATTENTION, READER!

TO READ BETHANY'S HIDDEN MESSAGE, TRACE THE PIECE OF PAPER ON PAGE 118. IT IS A FULL SIZE COPY OF THE PAPER EDWARD FOUND INSIDE OF THE CHESS PIECE DURING THE TOURNAMENT. CUT OUT THE HOLES.

THEN PLACE IT OVER BETHANY'S NOTE ON PAGE 19.

—GHOSTWRITER

8

The Lost Stove

LENNI READ OUT THE SECRET MESSAGE: "The money is in your hand."

They all studied the note, turning it over and over. "What could be so valuable about this piece of paper?" Lenni asked.

"It sure doesn't look like it's worth ten thousand dollars," Alex agreed.

"Read it out loud," suggested Jamal.

Lenni started reading. She stopped when she came to the word *declaration*. "What's that mean, exactly?" she asked.

"Oh, you know," Alex said. "A declaration is . . . is . . ."

Jamal headed for the dictionary on his shelf.

He found *declaration* and started reading off the definitions. The last definition was, "The document containing such a declaration."

"Like the Declaration of Independence," said Alex. "That was in your pile of American history books, Lenni. Lenni? You've been reading those books, haven't you?"

Lenni blushed. "I've been *planning* to."

"Same thing," Jamal joked.

"Be serious," Alex said. "This is the second clue about American history. What does that tell us?"

▶ **Junk Dirs (D)**

A A A Junk Collectors, 189 Av C----------------228–3900 ✗
A & A SCRAP Inc.

WE'LL HAUL ANYTHING METAL
TOP PRICES PAID

18–30 43 St--------------------------------- 730–8017 ✗

Bob's Junk, 74 Elizabeth----------------------- 781–8940 ✗
Collectors Inc., 88 Garden------------------------ 221–7553 ✗
Dave the Garbage Man, 1400 Prince------------ 684–2159 ✗
Gribaldi and Sons, 50 E 5---------------------- 226–3604 no answer
Newman Junk, 201 Morgan Av--------------------- 366–0718 busy
Ollie's Haul-away, 309 3 Av----------------------- 221–7430 ✗
Pete's Odds 'n' Ends, 22 Glavine Av------------- 781–3902
Quick Removal Inc., 3 Clinton---------------------- 230–8130
The Salvage Co., 11 E 18---------------------------- 226–3312
United Collectors, 66 Jay----------------------------- 330–3944
Winner Take All, 4 Ivy Ln----------------------------- 221–9434

"That the answer to this mystery has something to do with American history," Jamal answered.

"But *what*?" asked Lenni.

"Is this Ollie's Haul-away?" Tina asked. She was down to her last quarter. "Yes, I'm trying to track down a collection of junk that I believe was sold to your company in the last couple of weeks. The seller was a Mr. Edward Franklin." She frowned and made a mark on the phone book. "I see."

When she hung up, Gaby was staring at her.

Gaby's list:

A A A Junk Collectors, 228–3900
A & A SCRAP Inc., 730–8017
Bob's Junk, 781–8940
Collectors Inc., 221–7553 no answer
Dave the Garbage Man, 684–2159 busy
Gribaldi and Sons, 226–3604 ✗
Newman Junk, 366–0718 no answer
Ollie's Haul-away, 221–7430 busy
Pete's Odds 'n' Ends, 781–3902 ✗
Quick Removal Inc., 230–8130 ✗
The Salvage Co., 226–3312 ✗
United Collectors, 330–3944 ✗
Winner Take All, 221–9434 ✗

"I'm all out of quarters," Tina said.

Gaby looked in her pocket. "I've only got one left. No luck?"

Tina shook her head. "C'mon. Maybe Tuan is finally off the phone."

They headed back inside. Tuan was not off the phone.

"Hey," said Tina, looking at the two lists. "I think we called some of the same places."

"No wonder they were so rude," Gaby replied. "You know what? I think this is hopeless. We'll never find that stove."

"Wait a minute." Tina studied the lists closely. "Maybe it's not as bad as it looks."

ATTENTION, READER!
COMPARE THE TWO LISTS. CAN YOU FIG-
URE OUT WHICH IS THE ONLY JUNK COL-
LECTOR TINA AND GABY HAVE YET TO
CHECK?
—GHOSTWRITER

"You're right," Gaby agreed. "There's only one dealer left to check!"

They rushed to the phone. Tuan was still talking.

Tina rolled her eyes at Gaby and mouthed the word *girl*. Then she screamed, "Get off the phone!"

"Hey!" Tuan snapped. "Be cool." But he said into the phone, "Listen, Kyra, I'm going to have to call you back, okay? There's kind of an emergency here, and—"

Tina was prying the receiver out of her brother's hand. "It *is* an emergency," she told him when he stared at her in fury. She hung up and then quickly dialed the last junk collector on their list.

"Newman Junk," answered a deep, gruff voice.

Tina went through the story one last time. Except this time, the junk collector on the other end of the line said the magic words. "You're in luck, kid. I got the stove right here."

"You do?" Tina stared at Gaby, whose eyes burned with excitement. "Well, don't sell it to anyone, okay? Until we get there?"

The man laughed. "Not too much danger of that. It's a piece of junk, remember?"

Still, she and Gaby ran as fast as they could.

Newman Junk turned out to be a dingy store on Morgan Avenue. Outside were boxes of old records and paperbacks that looked like they had been rained on. Tina and Gaby went in.

The store was empty. Of people, anyway. It was filled, wall to wall, with junk—everything from old sofas to boxes filled with used light bulbs. Then a huge man in a T-shirt emerged through the beaded curtain at the back of the store. He was carrying a stuffed moose head.

"How can I help you?" He put the moose head down on the counter.

"My name is Tina Nguyen," Tina explained. "I called before, about Bethany Franklin's stove."

"Oh, yeah, it's right over here." He lifted a box of old magazines and two familiar watercolors (Bethany's!). Then he shoved aside a ratty old carpet. Underneath was the strange-looking old stove from Bethany's apartment. Then he went back behind the counter and started wiping dust off the moose.

Gaby fell on her knees in front of the stove. The old metal door creaked as it opened.

She peered inside. She felt around with both hands.

Her hands got covered with soot.

She didn't find a thing.

Gaby fell back. "Empty!" she groaned.

"I don't believe it," Tina said. "Let me check." She got down on her knees and searched as well, with the same results.

"All that work for nothing," said Gaby, wiping her sooty hands on her pants.

"Not interested after all?" the storekeeper asked them as they trooped out.

"No, thanks," Tina said. "It wasn't . . . what we expected."

"Yeah," the man said, not looking up from the moose head. "I couldn't really understand all the interest in that stove myself. I mean, it's not even an original. It's just a worthless old copy. And this is the second time in the last ten minutes that someone's been here to see it."

Tina and Gaby stopped dead in their tracks. They turned slowly back toward the counter. "The *second* time?" Gaby asked.

"Who was here before us?" Tina asked.

The junk dealer looked up. "Let's see. He was short. Bald. Three-piece suit. Friendly-looking. Smiled a lot, you know?"

"I do know," said Gaby. "That's Mr. Kohegan."

Dotting the
Final
i

"MR. KOHEGAN?" JAMAL SIGNALED TO HIS friends for quiet as he clutched the phone. "This is Jamal Jenkins calling."

"Call me Jason," the lawyer insisted. "Hello, Jamal. How are you?"

"Good. I think we have something."

"Again?"

Jamal explained about the hidden message.

"I don't know," Jason said. "Maybe you have got something this time. I'll tell you what. Why don't you bring over the note. I'll have it checked out."

"Terrific, thanks." Jamal hung up. He still had his hand on the receiver when the phone rang.

"Jamal," gushed Gaby, "it's—Kohegan."

"What? What is?"

"Kohegan—he was here—and—"

"Slow down."

"He's—a traitor. He's after—the money—"

Gaby had run to the nearest pay phone, and she was still out of breath.

A moment later, Jamal hung up the phone slowly. He bit his lower lip. "We've been betrayed," he said quietly. Then he told his friends the news.

"And now," Alex pointed out, "Kohegan knows that it's the note that's valuable."

"And he'll probably come after it," Jamal said. He looked at the piece of paper in Lenni's hands.

"Maybe we should put it in the bank," suggested Alex.

"Take it to the police," said Lenni.

"And say what?" asked Jamal.

"I could hide it in my house," Alex offered.

Suddenly, Lenni put down the note and yanked a notebook out of her book bag. She picked up Jamal's ruler and started measuring.

"What are you doing?" Jamal asked.

"I've got a better idea," she said. She measured a three-by-five piece of paper and snipped it out with Jamal's scissors. Then she put the paper over Bethany's note and started to trace.

"I'll make an identical copy for everyone in

the group," she explained. "Alex, you keep the original. Jamal, you keep a fake. I'll keep a fake, too, and so will Gaby. That way, if Edward or Kohegan tries to take the note from Jamal, all he'll get is a worthless piece of paper."

"Brilliant!" said Alex.

"There's only one thing," Jamal said, looking over her shoulder. "Let's hope the original isn't a worthless piece of paper, too."

May 3, 3:45.

Dear diary,

Things sure have been exciting lately. Yesterday, we found out that Bethany's lawyer is

Lenni dotted the *i*. Then she stopped writing. She stared at her diary. Something had just jogged her memory.

She was home alone, after school. She crossed to the kitchen, picked up a chocolate chip cookie off the plate her father had left out for her. Munching, she headed across the room to her backpack, which she had left under her electronic keyboard. She found her copy of the note.

When she had copied the note yesterday, she had tried to copy every mark, every scratch, every dot.

That's what dotting the *i* had just reminded her

of. Those dots in Bethany's note. What could they mean? Could they be some kind of code?

"Maybe it has something to do with the words that the dots are over," Lenni mused. She was thinking about the sheet of paper with the holes in it in the black rook. Maybe there was another hidden message in her note!

She opened her notebook, slipped off the pen that hung around her neck, and copied out all the dotted words:

DOESN'T BIGGEST YOU COULD ONLY LEFT THE PLEASE JUST NOT HAND ME GREAT PLEASURE BEAT- ING SON SET PLAYED! GROWN OF RATHER RIDING SO.

Lenni stared at the message. She couldn't make any sense out of it.

Suddenly the letters danced.

LENNI, ARE YOU ALL RIGHT? Ghostwriter spelled out. I CAN'T UNDERSTAND A WORD YOU'RE SAYING.

Lenni laughed. She wrote out what she was up to. A moment later, Ghostwriter was writing back, but Lenni was studying Bethany's note and didn't see.

ATTENTION, READER!
I THINK LENNI'S RIGHT. THE DOTS *ARE*
A CODE. TURN BACK TO BETHANY'S NOTE
ON PAGE 19. CAN YOU CRACK IT?
—GHOSTWRITER

Lenni studied the dots in the note. If they were
meant only to mark words, why were some dots
over the beginning of the word, some dots over
the middle of the word, and some dots over the
end of the word?

Could the dots be marking *letters*?

Lenni wrote out the dotted letters, and got this:

STUDYTHEUNDERLINEDWORDS

She broke it up into words.

STUDY THE UNDERLINED WORDS

Now her letters scrambled themselves. YES, wrote back Ghostwriter.

But the underlined words had led Gaby and Tina to the empty stove. She studied the note.

She copied over the underlined words:

STOVE, KITE, KEY, BIFOCALS, DEC-LARATION

OKAY, GHOSTWRITER, she wrote. NOW WHAT?

I'M AFRAID I'M IN THE DARK.

C'MON! Lenni scrawled.

I DON'T KNOW. LET ME CHECK MY LIST OF CLUES.

Lenni stared at the notebook page, waiting for Ghostwriter to return. Finally, the letters began to rearrange themselves once again.

AMERICAN HISTORY, Ghostwriter wrote.

HUH? WHAT ABOUT IT?

MAYBE IT'S THE MISSING PIECE IN THE PICTURE.

American history. Lenni sighed. She looked across the room at the pile of unopened books she had taken out of the library. It seemed there was no way around it. She was going to have to do some studying.

Just then, the doorbell rang. "Saved by the bell," Lenni said aloud. She looked through the peephole. Then she opened the two locks and let in Gaby and Tina.

"What's going on?" Gaby asked her.

"Plenty. Come on." She headed back toward the stack of books and showed them her discovery.

"See?" Gaby said, picking up one of the history books. "Alex was right. You should have read these books."

"Gaby, please," Lenni said. "You sound like my teachers."

"We could split the books up among the three of us and read them fast," Tina suggested. "Let's see. You've got six books here. That's—"

Lenni groaned. "Two whole books each. Do we have to read the whole thing?"

"Lenni's right," Gaby said. "It would help if we could focus on some particular period in American history."

Lenni started flipping through the pages of the book she was holding. Then she remembered. "The Declaration of Independence," she said.

"Huh? What about it?" Tina asked.

Lenni showed Tina the note, and the word *declaration*. "The word kind of sticks out," she pointed out. "Remember? We thought it might be another clue."

Gaby was checking the index of one of the books. "Page one-fifty-nine." She turned the pages until she came to a two-page illustration of the signing of the Declaration.

Lenni read over her shoulder. "You know, I hate to admit it. But this stuff's pretty interesting."

Gaby didn't look up.

She felt a strange prickling that seemed to race right over her scalp and down her back.

One of the names in the caption.

It had just jumped out at her.

And this name made sense out of all the underlined words. . . .

Cashing in
the Treasure

"BENJAMIN FRANKLIN !" GABY SHOUTED
out the name.

"What?" said Tina and Lenni in unison.

"Benjamin Franklin! Benjamin Franklin!"
Gaby clapped the book shut. "It all makes sense
now!"

"What does?" Lenni said.

"In one of Franklin's famous experiments, he
flew a kite with a key," Gaby said.

"Why?" asked Tina.

Gaby thought for a second. "Something to do
with electricity. I don't remember exactly," she
said. "But that doesn't matter now."

Tina looked at Bethany's note. "Okay. That
would explain *kite* and *key*. How about *bifocals*?"

"That's just it," Gaby said, her eyes shining. "Franklin *invented* bifocals. And he wore them, too."

"How do you know all this?" Lenni demanded. "Did you read these books?"

"No, but I've read other ones," Gaby said modestly.

"What about the stove?" Tina asked. "That word cost us a whole afternoon."

"I know," Gaby said. "But it was just another hint telling us about Franklin. The Franklin stove. That was another one of his inventions."

She looked in the index and turned to another page. "See?" She showed them the picture. There was the funny-looking stove that Gaby had sat on. "It's just like the one in Bethany's apartment, right?"

"Okay," said Lenni slowly. "I'm convinced you've solved the mystery. But where does that leave us? I mean, where's the money?"

They all stared at the note. Gaby's face fell. Could she be wrong?

ATTENTION, READER!

GABY ISN'T WRONG. BETHANY'S NOTE
IS WORTH $10,000!

HINT: LOOK AGAIN AT BETHANY'S
HANDWRITING IN HER NOTE TO JAMAL
ON PAGE 20.

CAN YOU GUESS WHERE THE MONEY IS?
—GHOSTWRITER

"B. Franklin," said Lenni. She looked pale.
She pointed to the signature on the note.

"The *B* stands for Bethany," Gaby said.

"But what if it doesn't?" Lenni asked. She
looked from Gaby to Tina. "What if it stands for
Benjamin?"

The signature was flowery, old-fashioned.

"Do you think—?" Gaby began.

"Wow," interrupted Tina. "An original Benjamin Franklin autograph. That would probably
be worth—"

They all looked at each other and whispered
the words at the same time: "Ten thousand dollars!"

They were screaming now, clapping each other
on the back, hugging each other, jumping up and
down.

"I've never held this much money before,"
Tina said.

"You still haven't," Lenni pointed out, hur-
rying to the phone. "It's a worthless copy. In

fact, you can have it. Alex has the—" She had punched in a number. "Jamal? Are you sitting down?"

Gaby screamed toward the phone, "We've got it!"

"Did you hear that?" Lenni asked with a grin. "Yes. It looks like we've saved the community center after all!"

"I called the police," Jamal told the group, as they waited at the bus stop. "And I talked to Lieutenant McQuade. I told him everything that was going on. Just in case Jason or Edward tries anything."

"You've got the note?" Gaby asked her brother again.

"Yes, yes, yes. How many times are you going to ask me that?"

"Ten thousand times," Gaby replied as the bus pulled in. "One for each dollar."

The autograph dealer that Tina had found in the Yellow Pages was on Third Avenue. The ride seemed endless.

On the way, Lenni was busy writing to Ghostwriter, telling him what had been going on.

FABULOUS! FANTASTIC! Ghostwriter wrote back.

But when Lenni looked up, her face was long. "What if we're wrong?" she asked.

"We're not wrong," Gaby said.

"That's what you said about the stove," Alex reminded her.

"I was wrong about the stove," Gaby admitted. "I'm right about this."

"Hey," Tina said. "That was our stop!"

Jamal leapt up and pushed the electric tape to signal the driver to stop.

"Why isn't the bus stopping?" cried Lenni.

Ahead, the streetlight turned yellow, and the bus sped up, zipping through the intersection. Horns blared.

"Stop! Stop!" yelled Tina and Gaby.

Jamal was staring at the back of the bus driver's head.

Something about that head looked awfully familiar. Suddenly, Jamal's blood ran cold.

He moved down the aisle, grabbing onto seats and poles to keep his balance.

The bus driver was a large man, beefy, and when he turned, Jamal saw he had a black-and-gray mustache and small, angry eyes.

But it wasn't Edward.

"I heard you yelling," the driver said in a surly voice. "But I can't stop until the next official stop, got it?" He parked the bus at the bus stop, and yanked on the silver handle. The front and back doors wheezed open.

"Sorry," Jamal said. He hopped down from the bus and joined his friends, who had all come out the back door.

"You look as if you saw a ghost," Alex told him.

"I wouldn't mind a ghost," Jamal answered. "The only ghost I know is friendly. I thought that driver was Edward."

Tina was studying the street signs and the address she had jotted down. "This way."

"There isn't any way Edward could know where we are, is there?" Alex asked as they hurried down the sidewalk.

"No," Jamal said. "At least, I don't think so."

They started to run, darting glances all around the street.

"Here it is!" yelled Tina. "'J. Parini, Autographs Bought and Sold.'"

The doorbell jingled as they charged in.

"Wow," said the thin man behind the counter. "Such enthusiasm."

"We've got an original Benjamin Franklin," Gaby announced proudly.

The man turned red. "Oh, I doubt that. Let's have a look."

Alex pulled out Bethany's note and handed it to the collector.

"How much is it worth?" Lenni asked breathlessly.

"That remains to be seen," the thin man said.

"But I mean," Lenni continued, "how much would it be worth, in general, an original Benjamin Franklin autograph?"

"As much as ten thousand dollars, I would imagine."

The kids beamed at each other.

The collector took a book off a shelf and propped it open on the table. Then he put on a loupe, a special magnifying glass, which he wore over his right eye. He peered at the signature on Bethany's note.

The group exchanged glances, as if to say, "This is it!"

"Forgery," declared the autograph collector, looking up.

"What?" asked Jamal blankly.

"It's a forgery," said the autograph collector, shutting his book with a bang. "And a very poor one at that."

A Desperate
Search

"BUT THAT CAN'T BE," LENNI SAID.

"No way," Alex said.

"It all made sense," said Gaby. "Stove, kite, key, declaration—"

"Wait a minute." The collector held up his hands. "I don't know what you're talking about. All I can tell you is that what I have here"—he crumpled up the note into a tiny ball—"is a totally worthless piece of paper." He tossed the paper into the trash bin.

"Hey!" said Jamal, "you have no right—"

"That's okay," Alex said, grabbing his arm. "We have copies."

"Oh?" said the collector. "More forgeries?"

"No. Copies," replied Lenni.

Lenni looked at Jamal, who looked at Alex, who looked at Gaby, who looked at Tina. It was as if each one had a light bulb over his or her head, and the bulbs all flashed on at the same instant.

They ran out of the store. The collector stared after them, totally mystified.

"But you said you gave me the original," said Alex as they raced back down the street.

"Well, I made a mistake, obviously," said Lenni.

The bus was just pulling out, but it stopped again to let them on. "We'll get all the copies and meet back at my place," Jamal said. "Then we'll come back to the autograph store."

When the bus ride was finally over, they split up and raced for their homes.

But as it turned out, getting all the copies was not going to be easy.

"What?" Gaby yowled when her mother told her the news.

Gaby had left her copy on the kitchen table. Her mother had thrown it out. Alex covered his face in his hands. Gaby fell to the floor, wailing. After a moment, though, she got up and began to search frantically through the stack of loose papers by the telephone.

Meanwhile, Lenni ransacked her loft from top

to bottom without success. "Hey, how about that? You're cleaning up," her dad said when he came in. "That's fantastic." But his face fell as she dumped the trash can out on the floor.

"So far nothing," Alex told Jamal on the phone. On the other side of the kitchen, Gaby was on the floor, going through the garbage with her mom.

"Keep looking," Jamal said.

Just then, Lenni realized where her copy was. "Tina?" she yelled, when Tina answered her phone. "I gave *you* my copy, remember?"

"You did?" Tina said. "Oh, wait a minute. That's right. You did. Hold on."

Clutching the phone, Lenni paced through her trashed apartment. Then her call-waiting signal beeped.

"Find it?" Jamal asked when she switched lines.

"Jamal, hi, no, but I just realized—hold on."

She switched back to her other line. She heard crying. "Tina?" she asked.

"I left it on my desk," Tina cried. "My little sister drew all over it. I'm so sorry."

"Oh, no," gasped Lenni.

"What if," Tina sobbed, "she just ruined ten thousand dollars?"

"I'll get back to you," Lenni promised. When she hung up, her phone rang instantly.

"Well?" Jamal said.

"Ruined," Lenni replied grimly.

"No!"

When he hung up, his phone rang before he could take his hand off the receiver. He picked up. "Hello?"

"We found it," Alex said. He sounded dead.

"Great! What's wrong?"

"It's shredded. We can't read a single word. All we have are tiny wet pieces of white paper."

"Okay," Jamal said. "I guess we gotta pray that my copy is really the one. Get over here as soon as you can."

When the group had gathered in his room, he said, "We're down to our last shot. Thank goodness my copy was right where I left it." He picked up his copy of Bethany's note, which was tucked under the base of his desk lamp.

Then something made them all look up.

Edward was standing in the doorway.

12

"Freeze!"

"AND MY MOTHER THOUGHT YOU KIDS
would figure out this puzzle before me," snarled
Edward. He chuckled. Then he stuck out his
hand. "Give it here."

"Don't do it," Alex told Jamal.

"Don't even think about it," Edward warned.
He took a quick step into the room and clapped
his large hand down on Jamal's shoulder. His
huge frame towered over the boy. "The note."

Jamal handed it over.

"I'll take that," said a quiet voice from the
doorway.

Edward whirled around.

Now Jason Kohegan strode in, holding his
hand out.

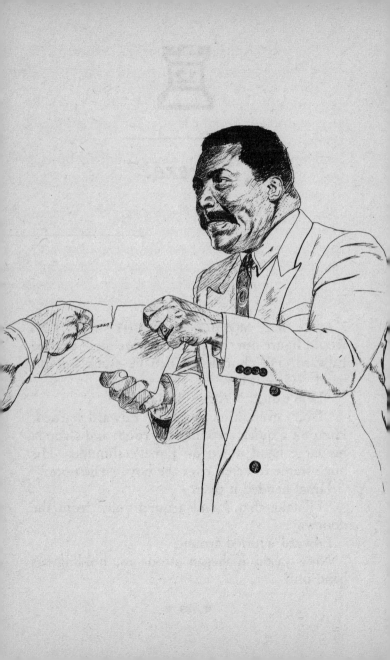

"No way, Kohegan. It's mine," Edward told him. "I'm her only son."

"*Now*, Edward," Jason said. "Look. The instructions in the will were very clear. You have to give it to me. I'm the lawyer for your mother's estate."

"Don't give it to him," Gaby suddenly blurted out. "He's just out for the money for himself!"

"It's true," the rest of the group agreed.

Jason Kohegan stared at them in amazement. "Now, you know that's not true." He was moving slowly toward Edward as he spoke. Suddenly, his hand flicked out and snatched the note.

But Edward snatched it back.

Both started pulling on the note.

"Freeze!" The tall figure of Lieutenant McQuade filled the doorway.

But they didn't freeze.

They kept pulling.

Rip!

Jason Kohegan stared down at the piece of paper in his hand, a horrified look on his face.

The priceless autograph had ripped in two.

Lost and Found

GABY HAD HER HEAD ON THE KITCHEN table.

"Now, c'mon, it's not so bad," Mrs. Fernandez said.

"Why not?" Alex asked as he trooped into the kitchen.

"Because," Mrs. Fernandez began. But she couldn't think of a reason.

"Mami, how many times have I asked you not to throw out my papers without asking me?" Gaby asked the table. "You threw out ten thousand dollars."

"Gaby," her mother said, "we don't know that your copy was the one."

Gaby moaned. Alex slumped into a chair and

stared at his mother angrily.

"How about I play you both a game of cards to cheer you up?" Mrs. Fernandez suggested. Her children didn't answer. "Hmm. I'll take that as a yes. Let me just clear this table."

She removed the sugar bowl from the center of the table, and then lifted the little red tile the bowl had been resting on.

Underneath the tile was a piece of paper. A three-by-five piece of paper.

No one said a word.

"You know what I was just remembering?" Mrs. Fernandez said. "I think I put a piece of paper under this tile for safekeeping. So maybe the little bits of shredded paper we found weren't the note at all. They must have been from the—"

But Gaby and Alex were already racing for the phone.

"You again?" The autograph collector did not look pleased to see the group of kids again. But the thin man's expression changed when he saw the police lieutenant who had come with them. And the policeman was followed by Mrs. Anne Ward from the community center. The collector put on his loupe and studied the autograph that Jamal handed to him.

"Well," he said, "this one looks more likely." He peeled off a tiny piece of paper that had been glued onto the larger note. "You see, this little

old piece of paper was glued onto this new note."
He held up the signature with a tweezers. "This
is what we call a cut signature."

"But is it real?" Jamal asked.

The collector bent down and studied the signature again.

There was a long silence.

Then he looked back up and announced his
verdict.

And the screams of excitement could be heard
almost four stores away.

The huge gun fired. A neutron torpedo screamed
straight toward his ship. Jamal swerved hard to
his left—and escaped.

"Nice going," said a voice at his shoulder.

"Thanks," replied Jamal, studying the video
screen.

The voice behind him chuckled. "No, I don't
mean Zargon."

Jamal turned. It was Anne Ward. He let go of
the video controls.

"Jamal, I just deposited the check from the
autograph dealer. I—the whole center can't thank
you kids enough." Mrs. Ward shook her head.
"Bethany sure gave you all some puzzle, huh?"

"She sure did," Jamal agreed.

"I don't know how you all figured it out."
Mrs. Ward cleared her throat. "Jamal, the center
can't really afford it, but I think it's only right if

we give you and your friends a reward."

Jamal's jaw dropped. "A reward?"

"Yes, would you accept a hundred dollars as a token of our thanks?"

"Would we accept a hundred dollars?" Jamal grinned. "Now, that's no puzzle!"

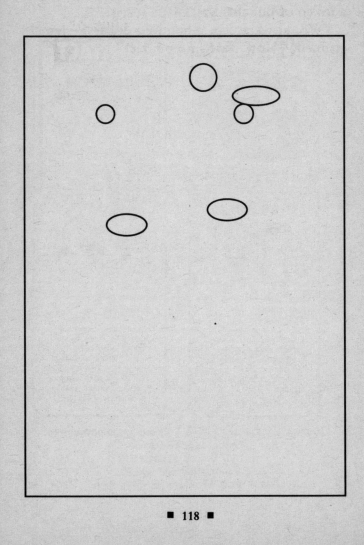